# Max In Australia

# Max In Australia

By Adam Whitmore
Illustrated by Janice Poltrick Donato

HAMLYN

Published 1986 by
Hamlyn Publishing
a division of The Hamlyn Publishing Group Limited
Bridge House, London Road,
Twickenham, Middlesex, England

Copyright © 1986 by Maxcat Inc

Produced by Acacia House Publishing Services Ltd

ISBN 0 600 31155 4

Printed in Spain by H. Fournier, S.A.

MAX is a big marmalade cat
with a fine round head, long bushy whiskers,
and big furry paws.
He is a very handsome cat, but one thing is wrong.
He has no tail.
Because he looks different from the other cats,
none of them will play with him.
Max sets out to find his tail,
and get it back from whoever has taken it,
so the other cats will be his friends.
He searches all over London, where he lives,
and when he does not find it
he goes to America, then to India.
When he still cannot find it, he stows away on a
plane to continue his search.

# MAX IN AUSTRALIA

Max slept all through the flight from India, lying in an overhead luggage bin. He had jumped up there when the cleaners left the plane and before the crew came aboard to get ready for the passengers.

He woke when the door to the luggage bin opened and a passenger reached up and took a raincoat. Then a flight attendant's voice on the public-address system asked all the passengers to stay in their seats, even though the plane had stopped at the terminal.

Max was hungry. He was very curious to see the new country too.

He wondered why all the passengers had been told to stay in their seats, even though the plane had stopped. Carefully he peeped out of the open luggage bin — and saw something that made his fur stand on end.

Two men in uniform were walking slowly down the aisle between the seats. They carried big spray

cans and were spraying everywhere.

Max had a dreadful thought. What if these men had come aboard to take over the plane and were gassing all the passengers? He lay low along the door of the bin, watching them come closer, still spraying.

Some of the spray drifted up and made Max sneeze. He crouched lower then, but no one had heard him.

The men finished spraying at last, and walked off the plane. Now, the passengers shuffled off. After they were gone, the crew left. Then it was very quiet.

As soon as Max saw the plane was empty, he jumped down and trotted toward the door. But on the way he passed a galley. It reminded him of how hungry he was, so he went in.

Max opened the refrigerator and found two slices of chocolate cake. He poured a glass of milk and drank it down. He was about to finish off the cake when he heard voices. Max looked down the aisle to the rear door.

Men in white coveralls had come on board, with brooms and sacks, and a big vacuum cleaner. They were speaking English, but their accents were not quite English.

Quickly, Max finished the cake and ran to the front, then looked down the stairs. There was no one around, and it was very hot outside, in bright sunlight.

In two great leaps, Max was down the stairs and on the concrete in front of the airport terminal. He looked up at the name on top of the terminal building. It

said ''Perth.'' Max knew from his TV travel films that Perth was in Western Australia. Now he understood what the men with the spray cans had been doing. Every plane that flew into Australia was sprayed with something that killed germs or bugs.

Max had always wanted to see Australia. Now he was here, and he hoped he'd find his tail. He knew there were many different kinds of animals here. Some of them were not found in any other country. Maybe one of them had his tail.

By now, Max knew about airports, too. The easiest way for a cat to get out was by walking around the back of a hangar and climbing through the fence.

That is what he did, and for a little while he sat beside the fence, watching the traffic. When he saw where most of the buses and cars were heading, he decided that must be the way to Perth. So he set off in that direction.

Max had walked about two miles in the hot sun be-

fore he stepped over to a cluster of trees for a rest in the shade.

"Good day, mate," a voice above him said.

Max looked up.

Halfway up the tree was the strangest looking animal he had ever seen. It had a coat of thick gray fur, a shiny black nose that looked like a small boxing glove, and big fuzzy ears. It was gripping the tree with the long claws of its hind feet and one front foot, and holding a leaf with its other front foot.

"What are you?" Max said, standing up.

"I'm a koala." (He pronounced it ko-*ah*-la.) Very

quickly the koala climbed down to the ground. "What's your name?"

"My name's Max. And yours?"

"Charlie. Charlie Koala. Pleased to meet you, Max. Where are you from?"

"England — but I've been to America, and I've just come from India."

"Is that a fact?" Charlie said, nibbling on his leaf. "Proper little explorer, aren't you, Max. What are you going to do in Australia?"

"Look for my tail."

"Why?"

"Because all the other cats have tails. They make fun of me and won't play with me, because I haven't got one."

"That doesn't sound very friendly, mate — I mean, Max."

"It isn't — but wouldn't the other koalas make fun of you, if you had no tail?"

"Not likely," said Charlie. "We koalas don't have tails." He turned to show Max. "A tail would get in the way when we climb trees."

"It's not the same for a cat, Charlie. I'm the only cat I know without a tail. Why do you climb trees, anyway?"

"To get tucker."

"What's that?"

"It's what we call food in Australia." Charlie held out the leaf. "My tucker's eucalyptus leaves."

"Is that all you eat?"

Charlie nodded. "What about you?"

"I like ice cream, chocolate cake, a little breast of chicken, salmon..."

"Sorry. All I've got are eucalyptus leaves."

"Sounds as if I'll have to walk into Perth to get some food," Max said.

"But you won't find your tail there, Max. You should look in the outback."

"What's the outback, Charlie?"

"Oh, come on, mate! I can't keep explaining these words. You'll have to learn our language, if you're going to stay here. The outback is the bush — all the wild country in the middle of Australia. Some funny animals live there — and some of them have tails big enough for two or three animals."

"Then I'll go there. Which way is it, Charlie?"

"A long way from here, mate, but it's in that direction." Charlie pointed off into the blue distance.

Max stood up and stretched. "I'd better get going then," he said.

"I hope you find your tail, mate!" Charlie called.

"Thank you, Charlie!" Max called back, stepping out briskly.

Toward the end of the day Max came to a stream. On the bank, he found some roast beef and cheese sandwiches that campers had left behind. Max ate them hungrily, then drank water from the stream. He slept all night under a low bush.

The next day he came upon a great herd of sheep. Those nearest him were standing in a group, nibbling the grass.

"Hello, mate," one of them said. "What are you doing here?"

"I'm heading for the outback to look for my tail," Max said, "but I thought I'd keep looking on the way."

"You won't find your tail here," the sheep said. "Look around."

Everywhere Max turned, there was nothing but sheep, and they all had short, woolly sheep's tails, which looked nothing like a cat's tail.

"Are there really animals in the outback with enormous tails?" Max asked then.

"Oh, yes, mate," the sheep said. "You'll have to keep on going and look for them."

"I will," Max said. "I've come a long way to find my tail, and I'll go on looking until I find it."

That evening, Max was lucky again. He found a frying pan full of lamb chops that some sheep herders had left beside a campfire when they went off to round up the sheep. Max ate them all.

The next day, in the middle of a large open plain, he saw a big animal sitting upright, eating leaves from a shrub. It had the biggest tail Max had ever seen. He was sure it was the animal Charlie Koala and the sheep had told him about. But the tail was even bigger than Charlie had said. It was big enough for *ten* animals!

Carefully, Max walked closer. The animal was light brown and shaped like a pear. It had two big hind legs and two smaller front legs like arms.

But Max could not stop looking at that amazing tail, lying out flat behind the animal.

Max walked around to the shrub where it was eating, but the animal did not see him, being so much bigger. In fact, it was about six feet tall.

As he stood in front of it, Max suddenly gasped.

On the animal's belly was a pouch. And hanging over the edge of the pouch was a small tail. Max sat staring at it, quite sure that after all his searching, he had finally found his tail.

This animal had back legs rather like his own: much longer than the front, and so powerful looking that Max thought it could probably jump just as high as he could. So it made perfect sense to him that the spare tail in its pouch was his.

Max jumped into the pouch, grabbing for the tail.

"Hey!" a tiny voice called. "What's going on?"

It was dark in there, but Max's eyes — like all cats' eyes — adjusted at once, and he saw a small animal just like the big one. It was upside down, looking for

something at the bottom of the pouch, and its tail had poked over the side.

"Who are you?" Max whispered.

"My name's Kenny. What's yours?"

"Max."

"What are you doing in my mother's pouch, Max?"

"I came for my tail. I thought your tail was it."

"Well, now you can see it's a kangaroo tail. And what are you?"

"A cat," Max said.

"I've never seen a cat without a tail," said Kenny.

"Neither have all the other cats. They think I'm funny."

There was a big bump then, and Max and Kenny were tossed about.

"My mother's moving," Kenny said. "Have a look."

Kenny and Max looked out over the top of the

pouch. Sure enough, the mother kangaroo was moving across the plain in great leaps.

"Do you think your mother could help me find my tail, Kenny?" Max said. "She can jump much faster than I can walk."

"Yes, I think she'll help. We can ask her."

"What's her name?" Max said.

"Kate. I'll give her the signal to stop, so we can talk to her." And Kenny tapped lightly on his mother's tummy.

Kate was very surprised to see Max, when he and Kenny climbed out. "Do I look like a taxi to you?" she asked him.

"No, ma'am," Max said.

"He's all right, Mother," said Kenny. "He's a cat named Max and he's looking for his tail."

"All the other cats think I look funny without it," Max said.

"Well, I don't think you look funny — and don't

you pay attention to anyone who does,'' said Kate. ''There are some who think I'm funny looking, but that's because they don't know any better. Some animals and some people are just not smart enough to understand anything that's different.''

''I'm sure you're right, Kate,'' Max said, ''but I'd still like to find my tail.''

Kate gave a motherly smile then. ''I'll help you, Max. Australia's too big a country for a cat to walk across. Jump up inside, little mate.''

The three of them went on for days and weeks together, across desert and mountains, and more desert. They saw many strange animals — from ant-eaters to opossums, from bandicoots to wombats — but they didn't find Max's tail.

One day Kate hopped to the top of a ridge of hills. Max and Kenny, looking out, saw the sea in the distance, with the sun sparkling on it.

"We've come to the east coast of Australia," said Kate, as Max and Kenny scrambled out of her pouch. "I can't take you any farther, Max. That sea is the South Pacific and there are towns on the coast where you can find a ship or a plane to take you somewhere else. We've searched all over Australia and your tail's not here."

"I know, Kate," Max said, "but thank you for helping me."

When Max had said goodbye to Kate and Kenny, he walked down toward the sea. There, on the wide, sandy beach, he found a bright orange surfboard. It seemed a good thing to lie on, so as not to get sand all over his coat.

It felt good to be still. Max lay on his back, closed his eyes, crossed his front paws on his chest, and went to sleep with the sun on him.

When he woke, he first thought he was back in Kate's pouch. He felt the same swaying motion. Max sat up on the surfboard and at that, all the fur on his back stood on end.

The surfboard was far out at sea, on top of a huge rolling wave. Far behind, he could see the strip of yellow beach where he had been, but it would soon disappear from view.

Max rolled on his belly and held on with the claws of all four feet. He could only hope that he would find his tail wherever he landed.